Fangs Menacing

May the Headlights Communicate

a book of haikus by Tonya Mae Howington

Book nine from the Cryptid Contemplation Series.

Sit. Read one haiku.

Let time pass. Stabilize and

immerse and simmer.

Enjoy.

tonya mae

he becomes the world

run rabbit run run run run

were-grizzly awakes

his strikes are random

were-tiger stalks his jungle

run rabbit run run

were-mouse not to be confused

his traps offer temptation

run rabbit run run

he makes grass whisper

run rabbit run run run run

were-fox doing tricks

run rabbit run run

he is a storm on the ground

were-elephant grey

he crushes the trees

run rabbit run run run run

were-eagle eating

were-boa strangling

his cavern of incisors

run rabbit run run

his speed creates chills

were-squirrel winter turns white

run rabbit run run

his hair is crystal

run rabbit run run run run

were-sheep charging

run rabbit run run

were-coyote is a ghost

he is gathering in dark

were-skunk emerges

run rabbit run run run run

he causes tears to burn

he pushes boulders

were-worm emerges hungry

run rabbit run run

were-moth draping wings

he folds night into a shroud

run rabbit run run

were-skunk pollutes hearts

run rabbit run run run run

he mocks with sad frowns

run rabbit run run

his faint familiar antlers

were-deer. not accord

he forces thirsting

run rabbit run run run run

were-camel shadows

he domesticates

were-bull is now the owner

run rabbit run run

were-dogs in a pack

he howls at the horizon

run rabbit run run

his big padded feet

run rabbit run run run run

were-panda hugs tight

run rabbit run run

he is sharp rocks on four legs

were-iguana scales

his black ringed spots bleed

run rabbit run run run run

were-jaguar lacks eyes

he whistles in woods

were-wood pecker hammers bones

run rabbit run run

his words are not real

were-rat scratches on the wall

run rabbit run run

he vomits green pus

run rabbit run run run run

were-toads in the pond

run rabbit run run

were-vampire-bat hunting blood

he seeks more than cows

his presence unnoticed

run rabbit run run run run

were-polarbear spreads

were-falcons homing

his master is death

run rabbit run run

were-fish encircle

he dissembles slowly

run rabbit run run

his trail cuts granite

run rabbit run run run run

were-snail acid slimes

run rabbit run run

were-jackal eats memories

his pack is monster

he is one of many

run rabbit run run run run

were-ants mark forward

his emotions rue

were-lion takes all control

run rabbit run run

were termite chewing

his crunching is getting louder

run rabbit run run

were-flea bite the bone

run rabbit run run run run

he bites to get large

run rabbit run run

he leaves leaving no traces

were-alligator

were-mink of iron

run rabbit run run run run

he is rare to see

were-firefly burn

he makes a late dawn hotter

run rabbit run run

were-dolphin stalk prey

he leaps high to pull under

run rabbit run run

he stretches limbs

run rabbit run run run run

were-tarantula

run rabbit run run

were-raccoon is masked

he washes his food

were-parrot chatters

run rabbit run run run run

he repeats terror

he flies in the sea

were- stingray stings like ice shards

run rabbit run run

were-centipede walks

he walks with dead patience

run rabbit run run

he is the full moon

run rabbit run run run run

were-armadillo

run rabbit run run

were-domesticated cat

he lives in houses

his bit mercurial

run rabbit run run run run

lead were-butterfly

were-black-widow says

his music raises the dead

run rabbit run run

leave no traces left

spots were-cockroaches gleans

run rabbit run run

he swallows trees

run rabbit run run run run

were-giraffe forest

run rabbit run run

he tempts with the pretty shells

were-hermit crab stalks

were-wolverine smiles

run rabbit run run run run

he is a razor pit

he floats obscuring

were-seal strikes from below hard

run rabbit run run

he is sweetness soured

were-gerbil in fallen leaves

run rabbit run run

he is running blind

run rabbit run run run run

were-wildebeest hunts

run rabbit run run

he waits mouth open wider

were-crocodile pearls

were-gnat is face close

run rabbit run run run run

he gets in the skin

he is visible

were-gecko green chameleon

run rabbit run run

were-vultures circle

he wants to witness the deaths

run rabbit run run

his nostrils flare fire

run rabbit run run run run

were-horse trots from hell

run rabbit run run

he is poignantly pointed

were-starfish migrate

were-scorpion shoots

run rabbit run run run run

his tiny arrows poison

he changes his stripes

were-zebra hypnotizes

run rabbit run run

were-cheetah resting

he throws the lightning faster

run rabbit run run

were-clam slams shut

run rabbit run run run run

he captures bodies

run rabbit run run

were-penguin is dressed to kill

he is cold as ice

his beak does not stop

run rabbit run run run run

were-rooster chasing

were-pig digs out roots

he chews every bone he finds

run rabbit run run

he is undeterred

were-caribou have ice blood

run rabbit run run

he is still hungry

run rabbit run run run run

were-panther eyes open

run rabbit run run

he has no mind for mercy

were-lamprey poisons

his teeth are jagged

run rabbit run run run run

were-opossum lives

were-chinchilla wraps

he is soft like broken glass

run rabbit run run

were-side winder slides

he uses his body rope

run rabbit run run

his arms reach the shore

run rabbit run run run run

were-squid climbs the waves

run rabbit run run

were-puffin breaks the whole rocks

he is cracking bones

his shadow blocks stars

run rabbit run run run run

were-moose heart is gone

were-duck congregates

he waddle has disappeared

run rabbit run run

he homes in on food

were-salmon climbs up the legs

run rabbit run run

his wool is flaming

run rabbit run run run run

were-sheep running wild

run rabbit run run

were-turtle strikes with its tongue

his shell is empty

his eyes are orange

run rabbit run run run run

were-koala clings

he blends into leaves

were-wren serenades to trap

run rabbit run run

he raises steel points

were-cockatiel is laughing

run rabbit run run

were-octopus walks

2rrun rabbit run run run run

he waves twenty arms

run rabbit run run
his red circles are acid
were-ladybug glows

were-carp slinks through ponds

run rabbit run run run run

he changes weather

were-rhinoceros

his horn is invisible

run rabbit run run

he swallows heads whole

were-gallinule sneers

run rabbit run run

were-screech owl has fangs

run rabbit run run run run

he screams with the wind

run rabbit run run

he grows as long as needed

were-weasel strangles

were-salamander

run rabbit run run run run

he is the under rocks

his legs are saw blades

were-beetles leave rips and tears

run rabbit run run

were-horsefly bites wounds

he does not die by swatting

run rabbit run run

he hits first with feet

run rabbit run run run run

were-kangaroo leaps

run rabbit run run

were-tick chews through bones with teeth

he consumes marrow

he splits waves open

run rabbit run run run run

were-orca rushes

his beak is a sword

were-pelican gulps then burps

run rabbit run run

were-manatee chomps

he takes all the time needed

run rabbit run run

he always impales

run rabbit run run run run

were-narwhale pierces

fangs menacing run

may the headlights communicate

were-wolf moon rises

J.F. and J.F. (2023)